For Matthew, with love and laughter —A.B.
For Lilian, Menno, and Hanna, with love —L.M.

Text copyright © 2011 by Ann Bonwill
Illustrations copyright © 2011 by Layn Marlow
Bug and Bear was originally published in England in 2011. This edition is
published by arrangement with Oxford University Press.
First Marshall Cavendish edition, 2011

Marshall Cavendish Corporation
99 White Plains Road
Tarrytown, NY 10591
www.marshallcavendish.us/kids

Library of Congress Cataloging-in-Publication Data
Bonwill, Ann.
Bug and Bear / by Ann Bonwill ; illustrated by Layn Marlow.
  p. cm.
Summary: Bear's best friend Bug wants to play with her, but Bear
is too tired and irritated to be nice to Bug.
ISBN 978-0-7614-5902-6
[1. Best friends—Fiction. 2. Friendship—Fiction. 3. Play—Fiction.
4. Behavior—Fiction. 5. Insects—Fiction. 6. Bears—Fiction.]
I. Marlow, Layn, ill. II. Title.
PZ7.B6446Bu 2011
[E]—dc22
   2010023118

The illustrations are rendered in gouache, pencil, watercolor, and colored
crayon on brown card.
Editor: Robin Benjamin

Paper used in the production of this book is a natural, recyclable product
made from wood grown in sustainable forests. The manufacturing process
conforms to the environmental regulations of the country of origin.

Printed in China (L)
10 9 8 7 6 5 4 3 2 1

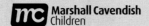

Marshall Cavendish
Children

Bug and Bear

by Ann Bonwill   illustrated by Layn Marlow

Marshall Cavendish Children

Bug was being annoying.
He zipped and zapped around Bear's head.

"Will you play with me, Bear?" he buzzed. "Please, please, pleazzzze?"

Bear didn't want to play. She wanted to nap.

"No, Bug,"
said Bear.
"I'm too tired
to play."

She let out a big yawn and lumbered off
toward her cave. But Bug followed her,
buzzing all the way.

When Bear heard Bug buzzing
behind her, she lumbered
faster. So Bug buzzed faster.

"Chase!" said Bug.

"Is that what we're playing?"

"Not now, Bug," said Bear.
"Oh," said Bug. "How about now?"
"Humph," said Bear and lumbered on.

Bug stopped to smell some flowers.
He counted to ten.
"Maybe Bear wants to play **now**,"
he thought. So off he buzzed to find her.

"Double humph," said Bear when she heard
Bug buzzing behind her again.
She lumbered faster
and faster . . .

so fast that she nearly
tripped over Chameleon,
who was hiding in the
yellow leaves.

Chameleon gave Bear an idea. She would hide from Bug! She leaned against a tree, thinking brown thoughts. But Bear didn't blend into the bark as well as she'd hoped . . .

and along came Bug, who spotted her right away.

"Hide and seek!" said Bug,

"Is that what we're playing?"

"Go away, Bug," said Bear.
"I want to be alone."

"We can be alone together!"
said Bug.

"That's impossible,"
said Bear.

"Oh," said Bug.

When Bear grumped
past Turtle,

he tucked into his shell
to keep out of her way.

Turtle gave
Bear an idea.

She would crawl inside
a hollow log to keep
out of Bug's way.

But Bear couldn't quite squeeze all of herself in . . .
and Bug could recognize Bear's paws anywhere.

"Follow the leader!" said Bug.

"Is that what we're playing?"

"No, Bug," said Bear.
"We are NOT playing."

"Oh," said Bug.

Just outside Bear's cave, Lizard was sunning
herself on a stone, sitting perfectly still.

Lizard gave
Bear an idea.

Bear stood still so that
Bug wouldn't notice her.

Her nose
was still.

Her arms
were still.

Even her ears
were still.

But Bear's eyelids were not still. . . .

They were droopy.

"Statues!" said Bug.

"Is that what we're playing?"

"Buzz off, Bug!" said Bear.
"Go and jump in a lake!"

And with that she humphed into her cave.
This time Bug did not buzz after Bear.

"Quiet at last," thought Bear,
as she settled down for her nap.

But Bear could not fall asleep.
She tossed and turned.

She tried counting squirrels.
Still she could not fall asleep.

"Maybe I should have been
nicer to Bug," she thought.

So she went outside to find him.

"I'm ready to play now, Bug," said Bear.

But Bug was not there. Bug was not anywhere.
No one had seen him—not Lizard, not Turtle,
not Chameleon. He was nowhere to be found,
and Bear was **very** worried.

"Bug is my friend," said Bear.
"I need to find him!"
"Maybe he went to the lake," said Lizard.
"Just like you told him to," said Chameleon.
Turtle nodded wisely.

Bear raced off to the lake and, sure enough,
there was Bug, floating on a lily pad.

But he didn't like being a water bug.
And he wanted to come ashore.

Bear jumped into the water.

She huffed and puffed her way to the middle
of the lake, scooped Bug up in her paw,
and placed him on top of her head.

"I'm sorry, Bug," said Bear,
when they were back on dry land.
"I shouldn't have said those mean things
to you. You are my best friend.
Would you like to play now?"

"I'm too tired to play," said Bug,
shaking the water from his wings.
"I think I'd like to take a nap."

And so they did.
Together.